Me in the Middle

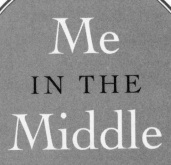

Me
IN THE
Middle

Ana Maria Machado

TRANSLATED BY
DAVID UNGER

WITH PICTURES BY
Caroline Merola

A GROUNDWOOD BOOK
DOUGLAS & McINTYRE
TORONTO VANCOUVER
BUFFALO

Originally published in Brazilian Portugese in 1982 as *Bisa Bia,
Bisa Bel* by Salamandra Consultoria Editorial, S.A., Río de
Janeiro. Published in Spanish in 1988 by Editorial Noguer,
España and in 1997 by Fondo de Cultura Económica, México.

Groundwood Books/Douglas & McIntyre
720 Bathurst Street, Suite 500, Toronto, Ontario M5S 2R4

Distributed in the USA by Publishers Group West
1700 Fourth Street, Berkeley, CA 94710

National Library of Canada Cataloguing in Publication Data
Machado, Ana Maria, 1941-
Me in the middle
Translation of: Bisa Bea, bisa Bel.
A Groundwood Book.
ISBN 0-88899-463-X (bound). ISBN 0-88899-467-2 (pbk.)
I. Merola, Caroline II. Unger, David III. Title.
PZ7.M1795Me 2002   j869'.3   C2001-902563-7

Printed and bound in Canada

Contents

Me in the Middle — 9

AT THE BOTTOM
OF A LITTLE BOX — 11

CHUBBY-CHEEKED
JELLY DONUT — 22

INVISIBLE TATTOO — 30

OLD-FASHIONED
CONVERSATIONS — 40

WHISTLING GIRLS — 52

A SNEEZE AND A TRAGEDY — 67

THE SOURCE OF THE
MYSTERIOUS VOICE — 78

PEOPLE BRAIDS — 95

"Would you like to know a secret that no one else even suspects?" Bisa Bea lives with me.

No one knows about her. No one can see her.

You can search all over the house, but you won't find her. If you look in the corner of a trunk or sniff under the rug or look behind a door, you won't find her. If you want, you can even look through the keyhole into my bedroom.

Will you see Bisa Bea?

I don't think so.

Do you know why? Bisa Bea lives with me, but not beside me. Bisa Bea lives very close to me. Actually, she lives inside me. I didn't know it until a few days ago. I didn't know until then that Bisa Bea even existed.

At the Bottom
of a Little Box

The first time I saw Bisa Bea she was very well hidden. I only found her because my mother was cleaning up.

My mother is very nice. She doesn't usually worry about neatness the way other mothers do. Sometimes she leaves things all over the house, and when she needs something, she drives us crazy, turning everything upside down.

But sometimes she goes on a real rampage. She does a general cleaning, as she likes to say. She cleans and cleans and cleans for two or three days in a row. She moves everything around, rips up paper and piles up the old clothes she never wears. She finds lots of things she thought she had lost. She tosses old magazines into the trash and gives me lots of paper to use in my art class at school. And she always has surprises for me — like the sparkling colored necklace she found one day and gave me for my costume box.

It was during one of my mother's general clean-ups that I met Bisa Bea. It was like the story of the giant that my aunt loves to tell. Have you heard it? It goes something like this.

There was a rock in the ocean, and inside the rock there was an egg, and inside the egg there was a candle and whoever blew out the candle would kill the giant.

Of course, there was no giant in my mother's general clean-up. No egg, either. But there was a pink candle from my first birthday party, which she kept as a souvenir inside my old shoe from when I was a baby.

But I am actually telling the story of the giant because I wanted to tell Bisa Bea's story in the same way. There was a closet inside my mother's bedroom, and inside the closet there was a trunk, and inside the trunk there was a box, and inside the box there was an envelope, and inside the envelope there was a stack of pictures, and in one of the pictures there was Bisa Bea.

I didn't know this at first. I came home from school and saw my mother's bedroom door open, the closet door open, the trunk wide open and Mama, sitting barefoot and her hair a mess, with a box in her hand. I kissed her and looked down at the box. It was the most beautiful thing in the world. A box made of different-colored woods, some dark and some light, forming patterns—a landscape with a hill, a little house, a pine tree and a few clouds in the sky.

My mother opened this box and took

a wrinkled gray envelope from the very bottom.

"What's inside it, Mama?"

"I don't remember. Let's have a look."

"It's full of things. The envelope's very thick."

And so it was, stuffed with lots of photos. There was one of a bunch of serious-looking people in a square. There was another of a whole family with lots of kids and even a little dog, gathered under the statue of Christ the Redeemer that sits on a mountain looking down over Rio. There was still another of a little girl with ribbons in her hair sitting on a bush that looked like a camel.

Can you believe it? I was impressed.

"Mama, how can a plant look like an animal?"

"Long ago people cut bushes into shapes. Some were round, others resembled chairs, still others looked like animals. This picture was taken in Paris

Park, which had a little pond and a foun-
tain that was lit with colored lights at
night. It was like a lit water balloon on
the ground."

"How do you know these things?"

"Because I remember, darling. I'm
that little girl."

"No, Mama, you're kidding…"

I glanced back and forth from my
mother to the photo of the little girl. It
was sweet to see my mother as a kid sitting on a camel's hump, thinking about a
water balloon. And it was strange seeing
her grown up, sitting in front of me on
the floor, explaining all this.

"We rode trolleys. It was so much fun.
Everything was fresh and open. Sometimes there were even two cars. We'd pay
for the ride and the conductor would pull
a cord and ring a bell. There was a kind
of clock way up high and the numbers
went up depending on how many people
got on the trolley."

I tried to imagine what that was like. I knew that a trolley was some kind of city train. Once I had seen one in a TV movie and I was dying to know more.

"Did the conductor have to let go of the steering wheel to pull the cord? Wasn't it dangerous?"

My mother smiled.

"Where did you get that idea? The trolley was the least dangerous thing in the whole world. The conductor had nothing to do with the steering wheel. He only made sure people paid. The motor-man was the one who steered…"

We were looking at the photos and talking when all of a sudden I saw the nicest picture you can imagine. It wasn't square or rectangular like the pictures you normally see. It was round and a bit long—oval, my mother later explained, like an egg. And it wasn't black-and-white or in color. It was brown and light beige. Mama told me that old pictures were usually that color, and it was called sepia. And the photo wasn't loose like the pictures you pick up from the photo store in a small album or inside an envelope. Not like that. That oval and sepia picture was mounted on a stiff piece of gray paper that had paper flowers on it. The decorations were kind of swollen up. It was nice to run your finger over the raised parts.

And best of all, right in the middle was a pretty little girl, her hair in curls, wearing a light-colored dress covered with ribbons and lace and beads. She was holding a doll with a hat in one hand and some kind of bicycle wheel — not attached to a bike and without spokes — in the other. It was a sort of metal circle.

"Mama, can I have that picture of the doll?"

"That's not a doll, sweetie. It's a picture of Abuela Beatriz."

"I don't know that grandmother. I

only know Abuela Dina and Abuela Esther. Are there others, Mama?"

"Yes. This was my grandmother. Abuela Beatriz. Your great-grandmother, your bisabuela."

"My bisabuela Beatriz…"

I kept staring at the picture, realizing that I couldn't call that pretty doll-faced little girl Bisabuela Beatriz. She didn't have a great-grandmother face. You only had to look at her to want to play with her.

"Where's the girl's doll, Mama? And what happened to the hula hoop? Did someone keep it?"

"No, this picture is from long ago. The doll must have been lost. And it wasn't a hula hoop…"

"It was a bicycle wheel."

"No, it was an old toy you rolled along the ground, trying to keep it balanced so it wouldn't fall over. It was called a hoop. It's from way before my time even, from when Abuela Beatriz—your great-grand-mother—was a kid," my mother said, somewhat wistfully.

"My great-grandmother, Bisabuela Beatriz…"

That was when I began thinking of her as my Bisa Bea. And I wanted her picture.

"Hey, Mama, can I keep the picture? It's so pretty. She's like a doll. Can I keep it?"

"What do you want it for? I don't want to lose it. You never even met your great-grandmother."

"But that's why. So I can take her with me everywhere until I get to know her. Take her to school, to the square, to all my hiding places. Can I have it? Please?"

My mother's voice got stiff. "No, it's the only picture I have of her."

But I made such a begging face that my mother took pity on me.

"Okay. But I can't give it to you. You can borrow it to take to school."

As I ran out jumping for joy with the photo in my hand, she said, "Please be very careful, okay? Don't fold it or get it dirty. And don't leave it anywhere. It's the only picture I have of your great-grandmother as a little girl. It's important to me."

I thought of stuffing the picture in my pants pocket, but it wouldn't fit. Only when I got to know Bisa Bea better did I learn the truth. She doesn't like girls in pants or shorts, not even nice ones. She thinks they're boys' clothes. Sometimes she has the strangest ideas. If it were up to her, girls would only wear embroidered lace dresses, skirts and aprons.

But I found that out much later. That first day I couldn't get the photo into my pocket and so I carried it to my room. I didn't know then that Bisa Bea had her own opinion. Or that she wanted to live with me.

CHUBBY-CHEEKED
JELLY DONUT

Bisa Bea went to school with me the next day, inside her pretty picture frame. During recess, I showed her to Adriana, my very best friend.

"Adriana, you have to meet this little girl in the picture. It's Bisa Bea. Isn't she nice?"

Adriana liked the photo, but she was shocked to learn it was my great-grandmother. To be honest, I think she was jealous because after she looked at the picture she said, "My great-grandmother is so different."

She had never told me she had a great-grandmother. "My great-grandmother is very old. She has white hair, glasses, old-lady clothes and she can't go out and play with me," she added.

I had to tell her that my great-grandmother wasn't around any more. She had died a long time ago and no longer had a little girl's face. The photo was from when she was very little. She'd only looked like the girl in the picture many, many years ago.

"So why do I need to get to know her as if she were still a girl? You act like she's alive."

"Adriana, she is alive. Of course she's alive. Do you think I'd walk around with the picture of someone who doesn't exist?"

"Hmmm...didn't you just tell me that she's no longer alive, that she's dead?"

But how could I explain that Bisa Bea really and truly does exist for me? I know that she died a long time ago and that back then, when her picture was taken, I didn't even know her. Back then I was the one

who didn't exist. I hadn't even been born.
But suddenly, from the moment I saw that
beautiful picture, Bisa Bea began to exist
for me. I spent a lot of my time thinking
about her, imagining her life, the games
she played and the things she made.

I couldn't explain all this to Adriana.

Just then Sergio walked up. He is the
nicest boy in the class—the most fun,
with the best ideas. I love talking to him.
Sometimes I think the two of us should
get married when we grow up. I would
like to spend the rest of my life looking at
him, listening to him tell me things, doing
things together. And I wanted him to
meet Bisa Bea.

"Sergio, look. Guess whose picture
this is?"

"I can't tell, but it's someone I know.
Let me see."

He looked at the photo for some time
and then said, "I know. I should have
known right away. But you look so dif-

ferent in that costume. It's obviously you. It just took me a while to recognize you in that countryish sort of dress."

What an idiot! Calling Bisa Bea's beautiful outfit a country dress. I was getting really mad at him when I remembered what one of my friend's grandmother says about men. They go around thinking about very important things, they are ignorant about fashion and we have to be patient with them. I always thought this was ridiculous. But her opinion came to my mind anyway.

Sergio kept on talking. He didn't even notice I was angry. "The difference is that in this picture you were fatter, with chubbier cheeks. But it's you for sure!" Realizing that our classmates were around, he added loudly, "Don't think I wouldn't recognize that jelly-donut face anywhere."

That really made me mad. Sergio is cute. There are times I want to marry him when I grow up, stuff like that. But the way he makes fun of me when his friends are around drives me crazy. He has this way of treating girls as if we were little nothings—acting as if I were a dodo.

I was so furious that I chased after him to hit him. I think he realized I wasn't joking, because he ran away really fast. He was laughing, teasing and shouting at me, but he never slowed down. He ran and ran. He was really afraid that I'd beat him up.

And then suddenly, when I was just about to catch him—not knowing what I'd do if I did—he screamed, "Don't lose the picture of that chubby-cheeked jelly donut, okay? I can put it on my bedroom door to frighten off the flies…"

Then I realized I had dropped Bisa Bea's picture in the yard. The wind was carrying it off. Hitting Sergio could wait. I couldn't lose my picture.

I turned around and chased after it. It was hard to catch. It seemed as if Bisa

Bea was trying to escape from me. The picture would land on the ground but the second I went to pick it up, it would fly away. Then it would settle down again, as if waiting, but as I drew near, off it flew into the wind. Eventually it ended up flying through the classroom window.

I went in to look for it.

When I walked into the classroom, I saw my history teacher, Doña Sonia, holding the picture in her hand.

"Come here, Isabel. Look at the beautiful picture the wind just blew in!"

I was glad she liked it. I started explaining. "I know. I was just coming to get it. It's mine."

"I love these old photographs. I collect them. This one is especially nice. Who is it?" she asked.

"My great-grandmother."

"Of course. I should have guessed. You look so much alike. Anyone looking

carefully would realize it. Your face is the same shape, you've got the same pointy chin—you're a perfect copy."

While she spoke, Doña Sonia compared the girl in the photo to me, glancing at my face, holding the picture up to the light streaming through the window. "Amazing. You have her very same eyes."

The bell rang when I was about to ask how my eyes could be hers if they were mine. Doña Sonia dashed into the hall, saying that she still had to find chalk before the class started. I had no other chance to talk to her that day.

I put Bisa Bea in my backpack, inside a book. When I got home, I finally had a chance to really look at her.

Invisible Tattoo

Every day when I come home from school it's the same thing. I throw my backpack on the bed, take off my uniform, put on any old playclothes and go to the corner to meet my friends. This day was no different, except that while I ate a piece of bread and butter, I examined Bisa Bea carefully.

Yes, Sergio was right. So was Doña Sonia. We looked exactly alike. It was as if that old-fashioned little girl were my sister.

I decided that she would go with me to the corner.

"Bisa Bea, do you want to come out and play with us?"

She didn't exactly give me an answer, but I knew she was dying to go out and play. First, silence means consent. Then I only had to look into her eyes to see how brightly they shone when I mentioned the idea.

Can you imagine? She must have been desperate to get out a bit, after spending all that time in the dark, stuffed in an envelope, inside a box locked in a trunk, just like in the story of the giant. Maybe that's why she had played so much during recess, flapping around in the wind, flying through the window, hiding in the classroom. That was it—Bisa Bea wanted to play with me.

The problem was she didn't want to go into the back pocket of my shorts. I tried to put her in carefully, but I couldn't. I tried very hard. No luck!

I realized that the photo was a little too big for my pocket, but it would fit if I forced it a little, crumpling the corners. Bisa Bea is a bit stubborn, as I'd begun to learn.

She went into my pocket, but since she didn't like it there, she complained and became very stiff. If I wanted to, I could walk and run, but I wouldn't have a good time, knowing that I had a pretty girl stuck in my back pocket—in a bad mood, face scrunched up. Poor thing! She had spent much too long locked up before my mother did her general cleaning. The best thing would be for her to be well protected *and* happy.

It occurred to me to lift up the front of my T-shirt and tuck Bisa Bea there, letting the elastic waistband of my shorts hold her safe and sound under my clothes, cradled against my belly and chest, where she could enjoy the warmth.

All these efforts made me late. When I got to the corner, the game was about to start and from what I could tell, we were playing tag, one of my favorites. I love running around.

There was no time to introduce my

friends to Bisa Bea. All I could do was start running, with her safely under my shirt. I'd have to introduce her later.

Run, dash, jump; run, dash, jump. The cardboard picture frame dug into my belly. It was as if Bisa Bea were softly punching me trying to tell me something. And little by little I began to understand what she was saying. "Hey, I don't like it when you run that way, playing kids' games. I think it's much better when you sit quietly and still on a bench like a pretty, well-brought-up girl."

I was having too much fun. I was in no mood to stop and give Bisa Bea explanations—the game was so exciting. If she wanted to punch me, I could punch her back. That way she'd learn.

"Be still, Bisa Bea!" I said, softly tapping her back.

I punched her, softly, so many times that she ended up staying still and quiet—just as she thought a good girl should be. And I could go on and enjoy my game in peace.

She behaved herself so well that I actually forgot about her. When we got tired of playing and went to get ice cream at the store, we were all talking excitedly. I forgot to offer her ice cream, although I'm sure she would have enjoyed it. I had no idea whether they even had ice cream back when she was a girl. Later I found out that they only had wooden iceboxes and they bought blocks of ice and put them inside. Bisa Bea only liked fruit sherbet and it had to be homemade. She still believes that the food we buy on the streets isn't safe and could end up making us sick. She doesn't call it junk food, but says something like "filling up with sweets from who knows where."

But that day I didn't know about all this. And so when we stopped for ice cream, I had forgotten about the picture of Bisa Bea lying snugly against my chest.

I only remembered when I got home — tired, sweaty and filthy, with grimy handprints on my collar. My T-shirt was disgusting. I decided to take a shower.

When I took off my clothes, I realized the picture was gone.

Where could it be? Had it dropped in the middle of the street when Beto pulled my clothes, almost ripping off my shorts? Or was it when I leapt over the wall to take a shortcut to the ice cream store? As much as I tried, I couldn't remember.

Just then my mother returned from work, came into the bathroom and asked, "What happened, sweetie? Did you take Abuela Beatriz's picture to school?"

"I did, Mama, and they liked her. Everyone wanted to see her. They even wanted to borrow her."

"Isabel, I don't want you to lose it."

"You can trust me, Mama. I will never lose her."

I said it so convincingly that I frightened

myself. I wasn't lying; I don't know how to lie. If I were to lie, I'd get completely confused and forget and repeat things, always changing the story. I think I'm a bit too absent-minded to lie successfully. So I answered her calmly, telling her the deepest and most honest truth as I understood it at that moment.

But then my mother asked, "So where's the picture?"

"You know what, Mama? Something very interesting happened. Bisa Bea really likes me. She liked going to school, meeting my friends, visiting my room and seeing my things. She wants to stay and live with me," I told her.

But she hardly paid any attention to what I was saying because she was already moving on to something else. My mother has a habit of asking questions and then not listening to the answers.

Still talking, I got into the shower. As the water began to fall, I heard my mother say something like, "Oh, yes, I see," somewhat distractedly.

"I put her away against my body, by my heart, in the safest place I could find. She really likes that. You know what, Mama? She wants to stay here forever, but she prefers being on the inside. Isn't that great? It was easy because I'd been running and sweating a lot, and her picture was damp and got stuck to me, just like a tattoo. She ended up painted on my skin. But not so anyone else can see her. Like a transparent or invisible tattoo."

I breathed deeply in the shower, waiting for my mother to answer. Since she said nothing—I don't even know if she was listening—I went on explaining. "Then she passed inside me, Mama. An invisible, transparent, inside tattoo on my chest. Now Bisa Bea is truly alive inside me. All the way inside." I turned off the faucet, adding, "She's going to live with me forever."

I stepped out of the shower. Mama wasn't in the bathroom. Another of her habits is going out and leaving you talking to yourself. Then she asks you the same question all over again. Since I had been in the shower, I wasn't sure when she had stopped listening to me, but this time it was for the best. She wouldn't ask me tons of questions about the missing picture. She might even forget about it.

But I would never ever be able to forget. Because now I, Isabel, sometimes called Bel, who has no brothers and sisters, had a special friend. A child-great-grandmother—a pretty, beautiful, adorable one—living inside my chest, with her doll, her hoop, her lace dress and all.

OLD-FASHIONED
CONVERSATIONS

That was when I started having long talks with Bisa Bea, usually when we were alone. She told me lots of things about her childhood. She showed me things, told me about her life and gave me advice—you can't imagine how much she liked to give advice. Sometimes she gave good advice, like when she suggested that I put these old-fashioned color pictures (she called them chromos) on the covers of my notebooks. We found some very pretty ones in the stationery store and I started a collection. I have angels, animals, children, hearts, clowns, birds, butterflies and flowers. I stick them everywhere—on windows, boxes and trunks. I put them all over my school backpack and save a whole bunch for my collection. One of these days I'm going to ask Doña Sonia to show me her collection of old portraits and I'll show her my pictures. I'll bet my collection is prettier. And this was all Bisa Bea's idea.

I told Bisa Bea all about Doña Sonia's collection and she told me that when she was a girl everyone went crazy collecting postcards. Every family collected them and showed them to visitors. Some people went so far as to put them in special display cases on furniture. People collected fans, ornaments and all kinds of things. It must have been lots of fun. I'd love to see those collections now, but I think you can only find them in museums and not in all of them.

Bisa Bea's ideas about furniture were sweet. She didn't know what closets were. Can you imagine? She was scared to death when she saw me open one for the first time. She thought it was a moving wall, a secret passage, Ali Baba's cave. She said they had armoires when she was young. They also didn't have TVs, sofa beds, blenders, sinks in the bathroom, cushions to sit on the floor—a whole bunch of things like that.

She also talked about other strange furniture with the weirdest names. There was a breakfront in the living room which she also called a credenza. It had a two-level ceramic fruit dish—a big plate on the bottom and a small one on the top—sitting on it. Can you imagine? She also told me there was a lace tablecloth under the dish because you always had to put a crocheted or stitched or lace doily under everything, I don't know why.

Her bed had mosquito netting. I thought the mosquito netting was a great idea, a kind of insect farm where you could keep and train mosquitoes to buzz whatever music you wanted to hear and

to sting people you didn't like. But she explained it was a cloth to keep mosquitoes from getting *in*, strung all around the bed like a curtain, because back then they didn't have the kind of bug spray that we see advertised on TV.

She also told me there was a vanity in her bedroom topped with perfume bottles and porcelain figurines. They were called *bibelots*. What a nice word. She said they were very pretty and that as far as she was concerned, I'm a kind of *bibelot*.

"I know what a vanity is, Bisa Bea. It has a mirror to brush your hair, right?"

"And also to freshen up...."

"Freshen up? Freshen your head?"

She laughed. Freshen up means to get ready, put on make-up, jewelry, make yourself pretty like my mother does in front of the bathroom mirror. Bisa Bea explained to me that bathrooms were quite different in her day. People washed their faces in their bedrooms. There was always a little stand with a washbowl and a pitcher of water, and a very clean towel on the side.

"And where did you make pipi?"

"There was a little house outside…"

"And if you had to go at night?"

"There was a chamber pot," she explained calmly.

"A what?"

"A chamber pot. It was stored under the bed or behind a special door of the dumbwaiter, as it was called in Brazil back then."

"A dumbwaiter? Didn't you tell me the other day that a waiter was a cleaning lady? Gosh! You people liked to treat others like slaves. Why did you need someone who couldn't talk to watch over the chamber pot?"

"Isabel, a dumbwaiter is like a little closet in the night stand. A secret, tiny room."

"A secret closet?"

As you've probably realized, Bisa Bea

and I can spend hours like this, talking and explaining things, as she likes to put it. She tells me about life during her time and I tell her about present-day life. Living inside an envelope, inside a box, inside a trunk in a closet, she has seen nothing of what has gone on all these years.

Food, for example, is a wonder to her. She knew nothing about frozen food or canned, dried, packaged and plastic goods and a whole bunch of other things. She had never heard of a microwave oven. Waves for her were something you see on the ocean.

When I told her one Sunday that I was going to eat a hot dog and drink a black cow, she went crazy.

"God help us, young lady! You eat dog? Poor puppy..."

You can't imagine what it took to explain it to her. It also took me a long time to explain to her that a snack was something like afternoon tea. She didn't know what a hot dog was, but she did know about sausage rolls. And a black cow? A Coke and lemon ice cream float? She had no idea what a Coke or any other soft drink was. They didn't exist in her time. And then when she told me what they usually had for snack or dessert in her house, it was my turn to cross my eyes and look shocked, while she sighed wistfully.

"Camel drool, Isabel, was such a treat!"

"Yuck! That is gross, Bisa. How could you eat that?"

"Angel breast was also delicious."

"A little angel's breast? How could you? If it were a chicken breast I could see it."

But then she told me about delicious sweets like gypsy's arm and mother-in-law's eyes and ladyfingers. Little by little I realized that these were names for different desserts. Get it? She was thinking I ate stew made from dogs and I was thinking she slurped camel drool. We speak the same language, but sometimes it's hard to believe. Some things have changed so much that it's hard for us to understand each other at all.

Even though I got confused, Bisa Bea didn't care. We had begun talking and that's what counted.

"My mother loved to make ladyfingers. Whenever she had extra egg whites, after using the yolks for other desserts, she'd beat the whites and make ladyfingers and put them in a *bonbonnière*."

Another strange word. That's how she speaks, often saying words in French.

"A what, Bisa Bea?"

"A candy dish. But instead of being made of crystal and filled with dried fruit, it was light green opaline and you'd put candies and caramels in it. It was so beautiful."

"And what's opaline? A kind of plastic?"

"No, love, plastic didn't exist back then. Have you forgotten? Opaline was a kind of almost transparent glass and could be made in any number of colors. My mother had a few opaline dishes. She had a blue *plafonnier*."

"You explained that to me the other day. It was a lamp."

"Exactly. And she had a pretty red brandy bottle in the shape of a duck. It had a duck's neck and its head was the cork—with a duck's bill and everything. She'd put it on a tray surrounded by a dozen crystal goblets."

"And what was it for?"

"For her many homemade liqueurs— crème de cacao and genipap, the liqueur made from the genipap fruit. She put them in the breakfront, which was a kind of cabinet for storing crystal and glass objects."

"They were all in there?"

"Of course. You could see the objects clearly because there were mirrors on all sides of the cabinet and the door was made of glass. But it wasn't plain glass. It was pure crystal. *Biseauté.*"

"Biscuit?"

"No, darling, *biseauté* was a kind of crystal carved into patterns and used for mirrors and windows. It's a shame it isn't made any more."

"Bisa Bea, the people during your time made everything so complicated. All those foreign words give me a headache. I bet you needed dozens of cleaning ladies to wash all those things and keep them clean. All without detergent, vacuum cleaners or washing machines! Just the thought of all that work makes me want to escape. Let's go have a snack."

And off we went, the two of us, as happy as can be. Or rather I went off, since no one could see Bisa Bea inside me, and I'm not stupid enough to talk to her out in the street. Can you imagine how much my friends would tease me?

WHISTLING GIRLS

As I've said, these talks with Bisa Bea can be quite amusing. But sometimes she can drive anyone crazy and sometimes I wish I could escape. But how can I escape from someone who lives deep inside me? Especially from someone who is invisible to the rest of the world.

What bothers me most about Bisa Bea is the way she is always giving me advice, as if she knew everything just because she lived so long—a long time without even TV, though. She's always saying things like, "Sweetie, I'm telling you this for your own good. You'll be big one day and realize I was right…"

Or else she says, "Listen to what I'm telling you, learn from my experience…"

"If I don't experience it on my own, how will I ever learn?" I sometimes answer.

I decided to put cotton in my ears when she was going on and on about experience. That didn't work because her voice comes from some place deep inside me. So I decided to make up a song and sing it very loudly—louder than her voice.

> Take a chance
> Take a chance
> If you don't risk, dare
> You won't advance, dance
> If you don't try
> You'll never fly
> Take a chance
> Take a chance

If I sing at the top of my lungs, her voice is drowned out. It feels like I'm finally the boss, doing what I want, without her interfering too much. But one day I had a sore throat, the start of a bad cold that eventually became a disaster, as you'll see. So instead of singing, I whistled.

Well, that was a mess. And Bisa Bea said, "Whistling girls and clucking hens always come to bad ends."

"Well, guess what, Bisa Bea? Every chicken I know can cluck."

"Well, guess what, Isabel? I'm sure that they all end up in the oven. Am I right?"

I had to agree with her. But even if they didn't cluck, they'd end up in the oven or saucepan, anyway. She didn't think so, because she said that if the hen didn't cluck, no one would know there was a loose chicken close by. And so no one would get the idea to have roast chicken for dinner. I had to tell her that nowadays people live in city houses and apartments, and chickens are raised on

farms before they make their way to the oven. We were arguing and all at once I understood that Bisa Bea had tricked me again. She was truly wicked. I mean, she always got what she wanted. I had stopped whistling and was listening to her again. So I thought we might as well talk about whistling.

"What's wrong with whistling?" I challenged.

"There's nothing wrong with it, my little darling."

"Didn't you say that whistling never leads to a good end?"

"I didn't say that. You didn't understand." Bisa Bea went on with her usual calm. "It's not the whistling that's ugly. It's the girl who whistles, who doesn't know how to behave and sounds like a street child."

Darn! Why did she say that?

All of a sudden I felt as if I had another voice inside me saying very softly but clearly, "Listen! Don't let anyone ever order you around like that."

That's just what I wanted to hear. I didn't even hesitate. I let loose with a curse (it wasn't a really bad word, it's just that any different word may sound bad to Bisa Bea's sensitive ears) and I ran out into the street, whistling and kicking whatever was in my way. I was being really naughty. I jumped up onto the top of the wall and suddenly I was watching silly, snobby Marcela in her best expensive outfit, flowered hairpins in her hair, sweetly saying, "Yeah, yeah, yeah," and smiling coyly at Sergio.

I couldn't take this. If I hadn't wasted so much time talking to Bisa Bea, I would have got to Sergio before she did.

But Sergio saw me and came over to talk. Since no other boy was around, he was quite friendly.

"Hi, Bel. What were you whistling? I liked it."

"It's one of my own songs. I made it up."

"I could play it on my flute."

"Great. I'll sing it to you very slowly."

That's when annoying old Marcela interrupted, "Have you seen all the guavas in Doña Teresa's courtyard? Too bad she's away on a trip! We could have asked her for some."

"That doesn't matter," Sergio replied. "Since she always gives us a few, we can simply go and take some. When she returns from her trip, we'll tell her. I did it once and she didn't mind."

"But how are we going to open the gate into her yard? Also, her garage door is closed," Marcela whined like a baby. "We can't get in."

"Why do we need to get into the garage? Are you planning to pick guavas by car?" I asked her. "Are you afraid to get dirty?"

Doña Teresa keeps the guava pole

with the little bag at the end in the garage," Marcela explained.

"But who needs the pole? We'll just climb the guava trees ourselves," Sergio said.

"What about the gate?"

"We can just climb over the wall," I said.

"I can't do that," Marcela explained. "My mother told me not to get dirty, not to get my clothes filthy. I'm too grown up to climb over walls."

I could hear Bisa Bea's voice rumbling inside me, agreeing with Marcela, remembering a whole bunch of things that a good girl shouldn't do. I whistled loudly while calculating the height of the wall.

But I could hear Sergio telling Marcela, "Don't worry, Marcelita. You stay here and I'll get you a guava. You don't need to get your clothes dirty or take a chance on getting hurt. Wait for me, I'll be right back."

Marcelita? What nerve! What about me? I pretended I hadn't heard and went ahead. I jumped over into the courtyard on the other side of the wall. Sergio followed me. Everything was fine up to that point. But then we heard barking.

Sergio shouted, "The dog's loose. Run quickly to the guava tree, Bel, or he'll catch us!"

Deep inside me Bisa Bea grew stronger. "Didn't I tell you? Girls who whistle end up…"

I barely had a chance to answer Sergio. "No, don't run. If you act like a scaredy cat, you'll make it worse. It's only Rex. He's my friend. Easy, boy."

Sure, Rex is scary. He's one of those humongous German shepherds! But he was my friend, and Sergio didn't know that.

Since Bisa Bea had come to live with

me, we were in the habit of visiting Doña Teresa every once in a while and having a snack with her. "High tea," as she and Bisa Bea would say. It was great! She would have tea or hot chocolate, home-made guava jam and lots of sweets, pies, crumb cakes, all kinds of cookies. She'd put out her embroidered tablecloth, round cloth napkins, a silver bowl, and so many things from Bisa Bea's time that she was very happy. Doña Teresa would break into a smile. She thought it was so sweet that a girl like me would waste her time with a little old lady, as she put it.

But we'd have lots to talk about, especially about the olden days. She was the only person I had kind of talked to about Bisa Bea, and I think she understood what I meant.

One day she went into her armoire and brought out an album full of sepia photographs and other portraits mounted in embossed cardboard frames (she's the one who told me that embossed was what they called swollen paper), and we spent a long while looking at pictures. Later she sat at the piano which had a candelabra fastened at each end. She removed the felt cloth covering the keys and began to play waltzes dreamily.

Bisa Bea was very happy. She almost wanted to come out and dance. While Doña Teresa played, I sat patting Rex's head.

Now as soon as Rex recognized me, he wanted to play. I only needed to pat him to calm him down.

"Hey, old buddy, it's me. Everything is fine, take it easy. We just came to get a few guavas, that's all. Easy, boy, easy."

I stroked his fur and hugged him. Sergio watched, his eyes as big as saucers. Then I told him, "Let's walk calmly. No running. Don't be afraid."

Soon we had climbed the guava tree. After we had each gulped down a few

guavas, Sergio looked at me and said, "Gosh, Bel, you are the bravest girl I know!"

I said nothing, but my heart thumped.

"And you climb trees like a boy."

I alone heard Bisa Bea's voice, "See what I mean? He thinks you're a boy. Men don't like that. Now he's going to think that you're a boy just like him and he'll take a guava as a gift to that neat and nicely groomed girl who is sitting patiently on the bench. Pretend you're hurt, silly girl, and he'll help you. Cry a bit and he'll want to protect you."

I was about to do as she said—it wasn't that much of an act because all I had to do was think of Marcela and I did feel like crying—when I heard that other voice, the soft voice that told me to whistle whenever I felt like it.

This voice now said, "No, don't start pretending. If he doesn't like you just the way you are, then he's a fool and he doesn't deserve to have you liking him. Don't do it."

I preferred this advice. I had no idea who the new voice belonged to, but I didn't fake it. I turned to Sergio, who was moving closer to me.

Do you know what he said next?

"You are truly the best and nicest girl I've ever known. You're not like those other girls who are always about to faint. Sometimes I feel like I want to marry you when I grow up. That way, my children won't have a silly mother like so many out there."

I had barely recovered from the shock of hearing that when Sergio stroked my hair and then kissed my cheek. My heart took such a leap that I lost my balance. Sensing I was about to fall, I reached for a branch and fell against Sergio. We tumbled down. We were in tears we were laughing so hard, hugging each other, while Rex licked us. I felt like crying with happiness. But I couldn't give anyone the pleasure of seeing me cry—not Sergio, not Bisa Bea and certainly not guava-faced Marcela who was waiting for us outside.

Remembering her, I quickly put on a serious face and changed the subject. "Don't forget about Marcela's guava. You promised her."

"You're right. I'll take her this one that fell. Only it's full of worms," he said.

"If it's rotten, go back up the tree and get her another one."

"Not me!"

And that's how Marcela Marcelita ended up with an old rotten guava full of teeny-weeny worms. And while she complained in her crybaby voice, I went home with my heart jumping and thumping. Each beat was a leap.

A SNEEZE AND
A TRAGEDY

I don't need to tell you that Sergio's words made me happy. But I can't keep it a secret any longer. It's not such a big secret, since Bisa Bea already knows. And, of course, she has offered me tons of advice. "A girl your age shouldn't be thinking about lovey-dovey things. That's not good. A girl your age should be jumping rope, playing house, playing jacks or making doll clothes."

"Aren't you always telling me that I'm already a young lady?"

"Yes, but that's a figure of speech…"

"And when you were alive, at what age did young ladies get married? Huh? Tell me, Bisa Bea."

"Well, I don't know. I can't remember. I've forgotten."

That's how she is. When she doesn't want to remember, she simply says she can't. But I'm not at all forgetful.

"The other day you told me that sometimes young ladies got married when they were thirteen. So I'm already old enough to start thinking about lovey-dovey things."

"But that was many, many years ago. Back then, girls didn't have boyfriends."

"They didn't have boyfriends? And still they got married?"

"Yes, of course. They married whomever their parents chose."

I thought she was joking, but she looked serious.

"Even today, it's very important that parents approve the marriage."

I heard another little voice talking deep inside me. It was speaking so softly that I couldn't hear a single word. But I replied,

even though no one had asked my opinion.

"Listen, Bisa Bea, do you want to know something? That was true a long, long time ago. Nowadays it's exactly the opposite. Girls my age or even thirteen-year-olds don't get married. But they can have crushes on boys and have boyfriends if they want. It's different when a girl has a boyfriend than when a grown-up woman has a boyfriend. But it's still a real boyfriend. And when it's time to get married, the parents have no say. Only the people involved. You see, we've figured out a new way of doing things."

Haven't I told you that Bisa Bea is nice? She remained quiet for a while and then said, "Listen, Bel, I'm not used to that. I have no idea how it works. But if you tell me that is how it is, I believe you, because a great-granddaughter of mine wouldn't lie. But there is a small problem."

"What's that?"

"If you want to have a boyfriend, sweetheart, you need to know how to get one. The way you are going about it is completely wrong."

I thought it best to cut her off right then and there.

"But it's working, Bisa Bea. I hope you aren't planning to butt in."

Since I asked her not to, she didn't. Well, for a few days at least. Very few days. By the time Wednesday rolled around, she couldn't hold back.

I had a very bad cold and hadn't stepped out of the house since Sunday. I was anxious to go to school to see my friends, especially Sergio, but I couldn't. Finally my mother let me out, bundled up, smelling of medicine and with a roll of tissues stuffed in my coat pocket. I was going no matter what.

At the school entrance, I walked by Sergio, who was talking to friends near the gate. Everyone said hi to me but I noticed that his hi was more like *Hi!*

I was so happy I could have burst. It was the first time he had smiled at me like that in front of our friends. I held in my joy and went to talk to Adriana.

"What's up? What's been going on without me?"

"Nothing important. Our math teacher gave us a pop quiz and all of us did badly. Oh, Doña Sonia asked me about you. She says she has a surprise for you."

"Probably a history test," I joked. But I knew it wasn't that and I was dying to find out.

While we were talking, our other friends gathered around. My heart was beating faster and faster, thumpety-thump, thumpety-thump, as if each of Sergio's steps were a beat.

Then a terrible thing happened.

I sneezed. "Aaaaachoooooo!"

It was loud! You probably think I'm exaggerating. Sneezing isn't a tragedy. Everyone sneezes when she has a cold or an allergy. I know. But this time it was truly a sneezing disaster. You see, after I sneezed, I really needed a tissue. I looked through my coat pockets but they were empty. My nose was about to drip—actually, it was already dripping, but I couldn't find anything to wipe it with.

I was sure I had brought tissues. But where were they? My nose was about to run, it was already running. The best thing would be to just disappear, but it was too late.

Obnoxious Fernando decided to pipe up, "What good did it do you to stay home all those days, eh, Bel? You didn't even have time for a shower. Hey, guys, look at her. Have you ever seen such a snot face?"

I was so angry that I didn't even think to tell him that snots are hard, or that mine at least stay in my nose while his can't drip out because they've replaced the brain in his skull, or something like that. But I couldn't find the words. I just felt like crying, or disappearing in shame and rage.

I ended up saying nothing. And I got madder and madder because as I tried to wipe my face on my coat sleeve—where were those tissues, anyway—all my friends fell to the ground laughing. All of them, including that two-faced Sergio—so nice when he's alone with me and so one-of-the-pack when he's with his friends.

I couldn't take it any more. I ran across the courtyard and locked myself in the washroom where I could cry and cry, with lots of toilet paper to blow my nose, as much paper as I wanted.

And there, between one sob and the next, Bisa Bea started talking to me.

"The boys in my day were very different, more chivalrous..."

What did that have to do with anthing?

"Were they more chivalrous at moments like this, Bisa Bea?"

She realized I didn't know the meaning of the word. "They were more gentlemanly...kind, educated, mindful of the ladies. If I dropped a handkerchief near a companion, he would quickly pick it up and politely bring it to me..."

I began to suspect what had happened to my "lost" tissues.

"Were you trying to help me, Bisa Bea?"

She didn't answer, as if she hadn't heard me. But I kept insisting until she finally had to speak, even though she didn't want to.

"Also, using paper instead of cloth handkerchiefs is a mistake. My handkerchiefs were made of linen and silk, nicely starched, and they had lace and embroidery."

I was seething. "Don't change the subject, Bisa Bea. They may have been prettier, but they weren't more hygienic. And I don't give a hoot about that. I just want to know if you were the one who dropped my tissues."

She confessed, sadly. "Yes, I did it, sweetheart, but with the best of intentions. I didn't know what would happen. When I was young…"

That's when I blew up. "I don't care about when you were young! When are you going to understand that things are different nowadays? I am my own person, I live in these times and I want to do everything I feel like doing, to live my own life. Do you understand, Bisa Bea? I'm my own person!"

I was so furious that I forgot my talks with Bisa Bea have to be silent, spoken to someone inside me so that no one else can hear. Otherwise, people will think I've gone crazy. But I had forgotten, and I was shouting, "I am my own person! I am my own person!" in the washroom.

A teacher who happened to walk by just then heard me. Luckily, it was Doña Sonia.

"What's wrong, Isabel? Don't cry, my darling. You shouldn't have come to school today. Poor thing, you must be delirious."

And so the school decided to send me home. I didn't even have to go into the classroom. They phoned my mother and told her I wasn't feeling well, so she would come to pick me up. I thought that would be the best thing. I wouldn't have to face all my friends. If nothing else, I'd make them feel sorry for having laughed at me. Good move.

THE SOURCE OF THE MYSTERIOUS VOICE

My mother took me home. On the drive back, we discussed a lot of things. I asked her what handkerchiefs were like during her childhood.

"They were made of cloth."

"Embroidered, with lace, and nicely starched?"

She looked at me strangely before looking back at the road.

"Yes, some handkerchiefs were very pretty. But they were difficult to wash, starch and iron. Some even had pictures embroidered or painted on them. But when paper tissues came out, I quickly switched. I thought they were the most practical things on earth. One of the worst things about doing housework was washing dirty handkerchiefs. Luckily nowadays we can do things in easy ways, so we have time to do other things. The handkerchiefs you mentioned were very nice, but that was when people had lots of servants in the house." She thought for a while and then added, "Also, I think they were part of a time when women generally didn't work outside the house, and chores were invented so that women could feel useful. Can you imagine how lonely it was to spend the whole day waiting for your husband and the children to come home? Lots of chores and no chance to do really creative work at home?"

I didn't understand what she meant. "Do you think a housewife's work is just invented, Mama, that it isn't useful?"

"That's not what I meant to say. I don't think I explained myself well. The problem is that it is work that doesn't change the world, doesn't make things better. It just keeps things the way they are. Washing to clean things and then getting them dirty; cooking to eat and then getting hungry again. I don't know. Of course I think that teaching a child is work that changes the world, but that's something a father does, too, and so does a mother who works outside the house."

I thought about what she was saying. Neither of us said anything for a few minutes.

She startled me when she interrupted the silence. "But if you are interested, I can show you some of those handkerchiefs. If I look through my things, I'm sure to find some embroidered ones. I have one of my mother's, with her monogram."

"Monogram? What's that? I've heard about telegrams. But a monogram?"

"A monogrammed handkerchief is embroidered with a person's initials."

I took a deep breath and asked, "Can I have it?"

"Yes, but it won't do you much good. It has my mother's initials, Dina Almeida, and your name is Isabel Miranda. It'll only be a memento for you. Whoever finds a handkerchief with the initials D.A. isn't going to think that it belongs to someone whose initials are I.M."

I decided to ask a question that I had always wondered about.

"Why is Grandma called Almeida and I'm called Miranda?"

"Because when your abuela married, she took the last name Ferreira and that was the name I was born with. But when I got married, I took Miranda as my last name—your father's last name."

"But I want to have yours, Grandma's and Bisa Bea's last name."

"You can't, darling. Each of us ended up with a different one. There are places where women keep their names after getting married. In other countries married women are just known as Mrs. So-and-So, by the husband's name."

"But don't my father, my grandfather and my great-grandfather all have the same last name?"

"Yes, on your father's side…because they are men."

"But I don't want that."

"Want what? You don't want to get married?"

"I don't want to change my last name."

"You can work that out later, with your husband."

But my mind was truly made up. "No, I've decided. I've had my name since I was born. My husband hasn't even met me yet. He has nothing to do with this."

My mother asked, "Why, Bel?"

"Because I am me. Why else?"

I liked my answer. My craziness, as they said in school. I think that my crazy answer will stick with me forever.

I remembered my handkerchief and went back to what we were discussing.

"Mama, would you embroider a handkerchief for me?"

"Sure. Embroidery is lots of fun. But I don't have time right now. Can it wait until after the competition?"

My mother is an architect, and she's involved in a competition to design a new hospital. She spends all her time in her studio sketching with her two colleagues. They walk around and around this huge T-bar laid over a transparent sheet of paper called onion paper (but it doesn't come from an onion) to make their final sketches. All I know is that until she is done with her design for the competition, my mother won't have time for anything. That's why I was a little sad, even though I knew it wouldn't do me any good. And I listened to Bisa Bea once again.

"Ask your mother to teach you how to do embroidery."

Good idea. "Mama, do you think you have time to teach me to sew? If I learn how, I can embroider my handkerchief on my own."

"That's my girl! We can put the time you have to rest at home to good use. Yes, I'll teach you. I promise you'll learn, quick as a wink. What a great idea!"

And so we began. Since handkerchiefs are very small, it would be too hard to make tiny stitches, so we started off by embroidering a placemat, doing cross-stitch, which is quite simple. I learned very quickly—a hill with a windmill and a Dutch woman on top, something pretty, with lots of bright and colorful flowers strewn on the ground. I counted the crosses and kept on sewing while my mother went back to her studio.

Bisa Bea was very happy. "That's exactly what a good young lady should do! I like to see a girl, my great-grand-daughter, working busily..."

I was still a bit angry at her and pretended I hadn't heard. She seemed apologetic. "My little darling, don't be angry with your great-grandmother because she dropped your tissues at school. I was only trying to help you. I wanted Sergio to pick them up and take them over to you so you could begin talking together and you'd smile at him. That was all…"

I continued embroidering, not answering. But I heard that other girl's voice that spoke to me every so often. And this time I paid serious attention. "Bisa Bea, please forgive me, but it doesn't work like that. Bel doesn't need to be coy. If she wants to speak to someone, she simply phones him up and they talk. It's that easy. Why complicate things?"

"Yes!" I thought.

The voice continued speaking, in a friendly way. "And stop being such a dodo, wasting your time sticking a needle in a rag just to please a bigger dodo who makes fun of you, just to pretend you are a delicate young lady. Why fake it? There are times when you shouldn't fake it. Put that down and go and do something worthwhile."

Now I got angry with *her*. "Don't butt in. I don't even know who you are and there you go making judgments about my life. I am not wasting my time. I really like embroidering, just the way I like skating and reading and dancing, watching TV, going to the beach, playing on the sidewalk, doing lots of things. And I'm not doing this to please anyone else. Just me." I thought about it a bit longer and added, "Also I'm not sure if Sergio is a dodo. Sometimes I think I'm stupid for liking him. Maybe we're both stupid. Other times I think neither of us is stupid—it's just the way we are. I'm not sure. And another thing. I don't want anything to do with people who butt into other people's lives without saying who they are. What do you want, anyway?"

I swear I heard a little laugh before she answered, "Sorry, Bisa..."

"She's Bisa, I'm not. Don't mix us up. And she's *my* great-grandmother, not yours."

"That's true. But you are *my* Bisa Bel, a beautiful girl, wearing a school uniform. I found an old photo in my mother's trunk, which I used to make a Delta holograph. The other one, she's your Bisa Bea, the little girl who's also there, in the picture in your hand."

I had no idea what was going on. How could I be someone's great-grandmother without knowing it? What was a Delta holograph? And how could I have a picture of Bisa Bea in my hand if it was lost? I knew it was lost even though I had come up with that nice story of how the photo became an invisible tattoo on my belly.

There are times when you can't really fake it. The girl had said that and she was absolutely right. Yes, Bisa Bea lived inside me, that was true. How that happened I don't know. But I did lose the picture. I know that. I can't fool myself.

With so many questions flying around inside my head, I had no idea which one to ask the owner of the voice. I ended up asking the stupidest question that came to mind.

"What's your name?"

"Beta. I'm your great-granddaughter. Nieta Beta."

Nieta? Granddaughter? No way. I needed to know what was going on.

"How can that be?"

"I live a very long time away from here. In another century. The other day, my mother, your granddaughter, was cleaning the house, putting her things in order, and I found an old picture of the sweetest, prettiest girl in the world—you!"

I was scared out of my wits. Beta continued, "So, we decided to make a Delta holograph and then…"

"Wait a second. Tell me what a Delta holograph is."

"You know what a photograph is, right? And you probably know that a holograph is a kind of three-dimensional photograph. You can turn the person in the holograph around and see her back, her sides, everything, as if she were real. Mommy explained that there were holographs when you were around, but you could only find them in a few places and you needed a huge special machine that took up a whole room by itself. But in my time you can make a holograph on a tiny machine that fits in your pocket. Delta holographs are holographs of old photos, paintings and drawings that weren't originally in three dimensions. I used your picture to make a Delta holograph, and I entered it. It must be a school photo."

"It can't be. It can't be true. No one ever took a photo of me holding the picture of Bisa Bea in my hand."

I was so sad I felt like crying as I tried to explain what had happened. "I lost Bisa Bea's picture."

"I don't know how that's possible. I know I saw her. And I really liked seeing both of you and that's why I came to visit, in spite of the danger."

Bisa Bea was scared to death to hear such things. All at once she needed to know what was going on. "Danger? What danger?"

Nieta Beta answered. "There was no danger if I just watched you both, quietly. But by speaking, I ran the risk that you would hear me, Bisa Bel. And then..."

"And then what?" I asked nervously.

"A little of me will end up living inside you forever."

"Next to me?" Bisa Bea wanted to know. "Is there enough room?"

"There has to be," Beta replied. "I think we'd better talk about this."

I liked the idea so much that I started clapping.

"There's one thing we have in common, my dear." Bisa Bea spoke up right away. "Both of us like Bel very, very much and we only want the best for her."

"That's true," said Beta. "But our ideas are so different. How will she ever know which of us is right?"

Beta was right about this. It's impossible to know whose ideas are better. Sometimes when I agree with my great-granddaughter, my heart goes thumpety-thump and wants to do it my great-grandmother's way, just for the heck of it. And there are times when I know it would be easier to follow Bisa Bea's advice—and make everyone happy with my good behavior. Then I want to do things Beta's way, even if it means fighting against everyone, knowing full well that it will be decades before anyone understands me. But whichever way, I am getting to know myself better little by little, and sometimes that's all I need.

PEOPLE BRAIDS

By the time I went back to school a few days later, I was starting to get used to my two friends, Bisa Bea and Nieta Beta. But just a little. There will always be a few scary things about this. Such as the idea of having a great-granddaughter. Sometimes people say that when they grow up they'll have this or do that, but you never really think that you'll have a great-granddaughter full of ideas or that you'll be a great-grandmother. I sure had never thought of it.

But now that I have, I'm more careful, so that Beta won't be ashamed of me or angry at me for doing things in old-fashioned ways. I got angry with Bisa Bea when she lost my tissues just to get the attention of a boy who wouldn't even stand up for me.

But there's another thing. When I start acting too sure of myself, when I feel so strong that I can face anything at all, I sometimes realize I am not Supergirl and have a great-grandmother relapse, as Nieta Beta likes to call it. That is, sometimes, when I feel helpless, I may want to be spoiled or need to be taken care of. Or maybe when I'm sad I'd like to be cuddled or get a pat on the head. I can't be Wonder Woman. At least, I can't be all the time without faking it. Slowly I'm realizing that I am a real mix-up inside.

The day I went back to school, that's how it was, a complete mix-up. I wanted to see my friends, but I was also embarrassed and afraid they would laugh at me again. When I remembered what had happened, I was really mad at them. My mind was all confused.

But no one even remembered the lost tissues and my runny nose. Everyone was talking about the new students—twins who had come back to Brazil after living a long time in lots of different countries like Chile, Italy, Germany and other places I don't remember. All the talk was about them.

"You'll see, Bel, how different they are," said Adriana.

"So are they Chilean or Italian?"

"They're Brazilian. Their parents were in exile, but they're from Brazil. And they've come back now."

"And how are they different? Aren't twins supposed to be exactly alike?"

"Yes, they do look alike. Just a bit, really. Like a brother and sister who aren't twins. But they're different from us. First of all, they speak funny, with an accent, a little bitsy accent. And sometimes they throw in foreign words when they talk."

"What else?"

"What else? They don't have cleaning ladies. The family does all the chores. That's how they like it. Can you believe it?"

At first it was hard to imagine. Sure, we know there are people who don't have cleaning ladies because they can't afford it. But by choice? Then I heard Nieta Beta's high-pitched voice. "Big deal! People who can't live without a cleaning lady are a disaster. Those times are over."

But since Adriana couldn't hear, she kept on talking. "They are really very nice. You'll like them. The girl's name is Maria and the brother's is Victor. They split the chores. Victor can cook really well, Bel. And Maria is a great plumber. She can even fix broken pipes. Everyone admires them. We all want to be friends with them."

Nieta Beta went on, "Big deal! I can repair my own things, too. I have a carpenter's table. I love engines."

But we had run out of time to talk.

The bell had rung, announcing the start of classes. On my way down the hall, I ran into my two new classmates.

Maria spoke first. "You must be Bel, eh? Are you feeling okay now?"

"I'm much better, thanks. How did you know who I was?"

"First of all, you're the only one in class who I haven't met and, secondly, because of the photo."

By then we were walking into the classroom and the class was about to begin. I would have to wait until recess for her to tell me which photo she was talking about.

It turned out I didn't have to wait. It was history class, and Doña Sonia was so happy to see me back.

"We were waiting for your return to give you a big surprise, Bel," she said. "Come here."

I got up and walked to her desk, dragging my feet. Was it a test?

"Your great-grandmother's picture," she said, handing me the photo.

I was so shocked I couldn't speak.

Doña Sonia went on, "You must have dropped it on the sidewalk when you were playing. One of your classmates found it and brought it to me thinking it was part of my collection. I recognized it at once and knew it was yours. I've wanted to give it back to you for days, but since you've been out of class, I had to wait."

I was still in shock. It was too good to be true!

"And I want to straighten something else out with you," Doña Sonia went on. "While you were away sick, I took pictures of all the students except for you. Today is your turn. At last! Come, stand by the window where there's more light."

I went to stand there to be photographed with Bisa Bea's picture in my

Reference 937-8221
Circulation 937-8416

Library name: ANGELOU
User ID: 20091030206

Author: Machado, Ana Maria, 1941-
Title: Me in the middle
Item ID: 020033661590
Date due: 8/3/2017,23:59
Call number: J MACH

Author: Schrefer, Eliot, 1978-
Title: Rise and fall
Item ID: 50000010994597
Date due: 8/3/2017,23:59
Call number: J SCHREFER E

Author: Kinney, Jeff.
Title: Diary of a wimpy kid : dog days
Item ID: 50000011414504
Date due: 8/3/2017,23:59
Call number: J KINNEY J

Author: Adler, David A.
Title: Cam Jansen and the school play myst
ery
Item ID: 020031110014
Date due: 8/3/2017,23:59
Call number: JM ADL

Tu 3-8, W 1-6
Th,F & Sa 12-5
M & Su Closed
-
www.ssjcpl.org

hand. Nieta Beta wouldn't leave me in peace.

"Didn't I tell you? That was the picture that was in my mother's trunk. You're wearing your school uniform, one sock lower than the other, those little braids, and holding Bisa Bea in your hands."

Very interesting. In a minute I was going to have my picture taken, but in the future the picture was already a memory for my great-granddaughter.

Doña Sonia took my picture. When I got back to my seat, she said, "Isabel, there's another new development. I showed your classmates your great-grandmother's picture and they all started to bring in pictures of their own great-grandparents. So we've decided to study the period in which they lived. We will spend a few weeks researching that period—the end of the nineteenth century

and the beginning of the twentieth. What do you think?"

I was so happy to have Bisa Bea's picture back that I couldn't say a word, especially after I heard that we would be learning more about the time when she lived. It was going to be great! I was tongue-tied and felt like crying with joy. I just can't explain it.

Then I suddenly realized that Victor, the new student, was drying a tear at the corner of his eye, although he was acting as if nothing unusual had happened. I didn't know why. What a strange boy. Didn't he know that men aren't supposed to cry in public?

Doña Sonia began class by telling us that when my great-grandmother was alive, there were slaves. The slaves had owners, as if they were objects, and they worked their whole lives without resting. They received no wages and they had no rights.

We had heard this before, but this time we were being asked to think about it.

When she asked if anyone had a question or wanted to say something, Victor raised his hand. His voice was choked with emotion.

"Doña Sonia, my heart jumped when you began to talk about Bel's great-grandmother. I started to remember my grandfather and now I would really like to talk about him. May I?"

"Of course, Victor."

"You all know that we lived outside Brazil for many years. I didn't see my grandfather very often because he stayed here, but I did manage to get to know him pretty well. When we went into exile, I was very small and I could barely remember a thing about Brazil. But my grandfather came to visit us a few times. We also wrote to him and sometimes we'd talk on the phone. He died when we were living very far away. I never had the chance to really enjoy him and that makes me very sad. I miss him a lot and I feel like crying now."

Wow. He dried another tear on his face. He wasn't afraid the others would laugh. That moment I discovered that Victor was the bravest boy I had ever met. He had the courage to cry in front of the whole class!

He went on. "I remember one night he came to visit us when we were living in Rome. It was the night before he went back to Brazil. Maria and I wanted to go with him. We wanted our mother and father to return to our country, too. We were all sad and weepy. I didn't understand that it was impossible for us to go back.

"Then Grandpa explained that one day we would be able to return, but that people who want to build a new society aren't often understood. They can be persecuted and made to suffer and that's what had happened in our country. He told us many stories about the history of Brazil and the world. He told us that during his lifetime things were much better than in his father's because there were no more slaves, and workers were paid. He could remember that when he was little, in his hometown, the workers spent fourteen or sixteen hours standing in front of their machines and couldn't go on strike. Even the children worked. He told us stuff like that. I don't remember all of it because the details get mixed up in my head. But I will never forget how my grandfather's eyes looked as he spoke about these things. I'll also never forget that that was the first time I saw my father cry, as he listened to my grandfather talk."

We weren't part of his family, but all of us felt like crying, too. Just from the emotion in Victor's voice as he told us about that cold night, a few years ago, far away from Brazil on the other side of the ocean, in conversation with an old man who was no longer alive.

"That day I understood that my grandfather would always live inside me," he went on, as if he were reading my mind. "After talking for a long time, Grandpa said that we should always try to improve things, in order to leave the world better off for our own children, just like our father who was a journalist and our mother who was a teacher. He told us that he was proud of our parents. Exile was a kind of price we had to pay for the future to be better. He said that there were many people paying that price and some were paying an even higher price than we were, but that it was worth it. So when we were talking about Isabel's great-grandmother, I started missing my grandfather a lot. I was sad that he died before we could celebrate our return. But I could also see how some things are better during our time than they were in his. And I started to think, What will the world be like for our grandchildren? And for our great-grand-children? I think we could research this, too. That's what I wanted to say."

And he sat down.

At first the classroom was dead silent. Then there was a buzz in the room. Everyone thought this was a good idea, to begin thinking about how the world could be made better with each parent, child, grandchild, great-grandchild. And how you could take advantage of what each person did to make things better — parent, grandparent, great-grandparent, great-great grandparent, great-great-great grandparent — until you couldn't even remember the grandparents.

To study the future. Can you imagine? Much better to be stuck in the past, the way most schools are.

"Good. We'll do it," said Doña Sonia,

ending the class. It had gone by so fast. "Each one of you go home and think about this until our next class. Discuss it with your family, your friends. Imagine, dream about it. What a great idea. This will be our topic — from the great-grand-parents to the great-grandchildren."

And then I knew. I figured it out all of a sudden. I realized that nothing happens by chance. From that moment, I knew that schoolwork isn't just done through books or outside me. It also happens in my own life, inside me, in my secrets, in my mysteries, in my doubts. Bisa Bea argues with Nieta Beta with me in the middle being pulled this way and that. Boys and girls have different ideas of how to act, and those ideas are always changing. I'm always changing, too, and that can be so hard you sometimes want to cry. Looking back at the past and walking toward the future, I stumble every once in a while, as I invent new styles. I am also an inventor. All day long I invent a new way of living.

I, Bel, am like a braid, just like the braids in my hair. I divide into three strands and I cross them one over the other—first my strand, than Bisa Bea's, and then Nieta Beta. And Nieta Beta will make a braid, using strands of me, Bisa Bel, crossed over her own and with that of her great-grandchild to be, whose existence I can't even begin to imagine. It will always be this way, better each time, better for each one of us and for the whole world—a people braid.

And that's why I decided to tell you the secret—to tell you that Bisa Bea lives inside me. But when I get excited, I just can't stop talking, so I ended up telling it all. Even Nieta Beta came to join us.

And the three of us will pass on all our strengths, from one braid to the next.